This book belongs to

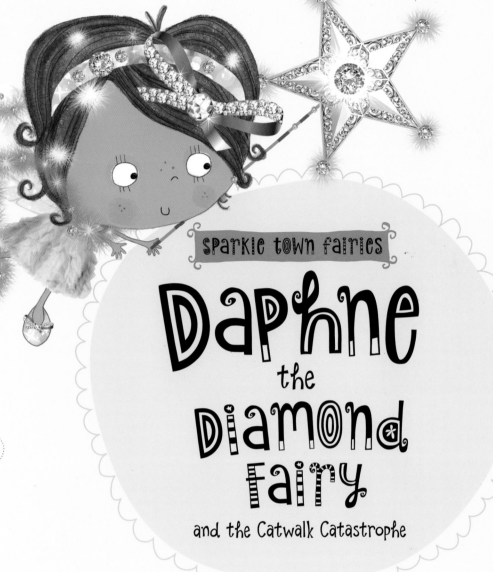

sparkle town fairies

Daphne
the
Diamond
Fairy
and the Catwalk Catastrophe

Sarah Creese * Lara Ede

make
believe
ideas

On **Sparkle Town's** main shopping street,
there stood a grand **boutique**,

filled with **dresses**, hats, and shoes
so cute, and oh-so-chic!

DIAMOND BOUTIQUE

Every **dress** was quite unique —
but one thing did not vary:
each stitch and style was made by hand
by **Daphne** the **Diamond Fairy**.

Diamonds
are always
in style.

The fairies flocked from miles around
to buy each new design —
at times poor Daphne had to shout,
"Please, darlings, wait in line!"

Ooh,
I love it!

MADE BY DAPHNE

MADE BY DAPHNE

MADE BY DAPHNE

First she sketched

and next she cut,

then it was time

to **sew**

in every color imaginable.
And lastly, for **extra glow**...

she swished her special **sparkle wand**,
and with a twinkling smile

Perfect!

there appeared a **dazzling diamond** —
her signature fairy style.

One morning Daphne left for work,
but as she turned the corner,

a letter carried by **Fluttermail** unfurled itself before her.

High Street

You've got mail!

"Dear Daphne,"
it read, in fancy script.
"We hereby invite you to sew
six dresses
for the one, the only,
Queenie Quartz's
Fashion Show."

Entry by invitation only.
Designs judged by Queenie Quartz herself,
head of Top Fairy, Fairy Land's most successful
fashion store ever — no really, EVER.

Flutter
Flutter

Queenie Quartz

Flutter
Flutter

Filled with glee,
she **whizzed** to work
to start her dress collection.

"It has to be my best," she said.
"**To win I need perfection.**"

All day and night
she **waved** her wand
but nothing seemed
quite right.

Swish!
Swoosh!

Then by chance
she tripped
and swished!

Swoo-oops!

From her wand
came a **wondrous sight**...

A shower of **glittering diamonds**, covering each and every dress.

Daphne blinked from the diamonds' dazzle.

This look was **THE ONE** to impress!

The next day, Daphne's friends arrived
to be fitted for the show.
Daphne revealed her new designs
and they **gasped** at the glamorous glow.

You look
dazzling.

No, you look
dazzling.

But seeing her friends look so **sublime**,
Daphne's thoughts turned jealous and sour.
"Why should **they** be the ones to shine
and steal my finest hour?"

Daphne, these are
sparkletastic!

Hmm.

And in a whirl she frowned, then **snapped**, "I'm afraid this just won't do. My **creations** are far too good – they'll look better on **ME** than you."

I'll wear ALL of them.

Soon, the **show day** came around,
and Daphne was well-prepared.

Her friends, meanwhile, sat at the back
(they were hurt, but they still cared).

Backstage, fairies flitted about
so no one saw Queenie's cat,

who chased a feathery bird
(well, a dress)

causing a **catastrophe** that...

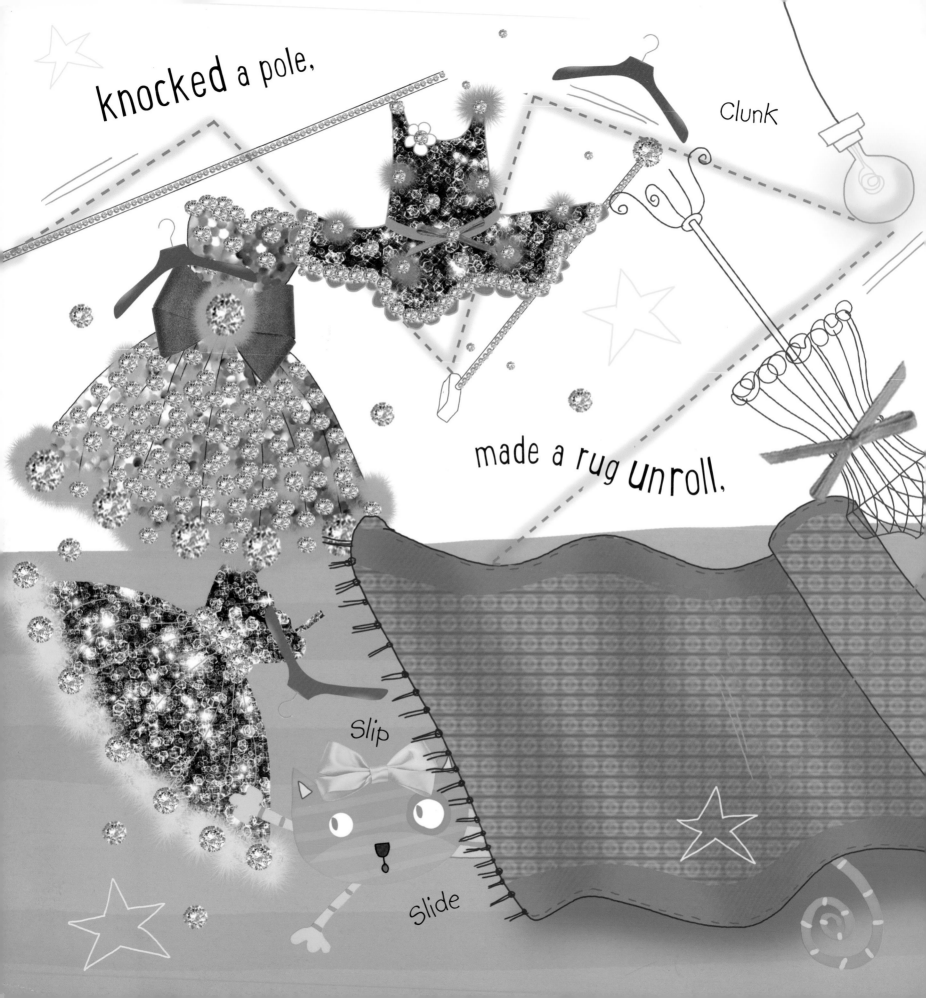

and toppled a
teetering tower,

which broke
a big switch –

← ON

a disastrous glitch –

Woah!

AND...

TURNED OFF ALL THE POWER.

In the dark, the fairies flapped,
but Daphne had an **idea**.
By wand-light, something caught her eye
and made the **answer** clear.

"I can't do this alone," she thought,
and **rushed** to find her friends.
"I know now I was wrong," she said.
"Can we ever make amends?
I'm **sorry** for being selfish;
it was mean and unfair, too."
The fairies **smiled**, then **hugged** their friend
and said, "What can we do?"

Here's the plan...

Wowzer!

She gave each friend a **diamond dress**, then told them where to go.
"Fairies at the ready," she cried, "it's time to save this **show!**"

Who needs lights!

Daphne swooshed her diamond wand — up high, then left to right.
She bounced a beam from dress to dress, filling the room with **LIGHT!**

The show was such a great success
that Queenie had to say,

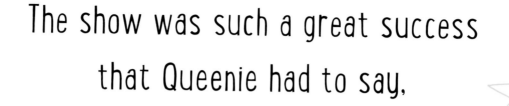

"Dear Daphne, will you come each year
to be our **light display?**"

And though the fairies' dresses
sparkled beyond compare,
the thing that **sparkled** most of all
was the **friendship** that they **shared!**